Published by
WonderCorp
Las Vegas, NV

Publisher's Cataloging-in-Publication Data
Tuttle, Alexa.

Rosie and Mr. Spooks / story by Alexa Tuttle ;
illustrated by Carlie Tuttle. – Las Vegas, NV : WonderCorp, 2018.

p. ; cm.

Summary: Rosie is chased through her house on Halloween night by a determined little spider, until she learns he wants to be her friend and names him "Mr. Spooks".

ISBN13: 978-0-9980230-1-4

1. Halloween—Juvenile fiction. 2. Girls—Juvenile fiction.
3. Spiders—Juvenile fiction. I. Title. II. Tuttle, Carlie.

PZ7.5.T87 2018
[E]—dc23   2018952099

Project coordination by Jenkins Group, Inc.
www.BookPublishing.com

Design by Alexa Tuttle

Printed in the United States of America by Four Colour Print Group,
Clarksville, TN, First Printing, August 2018, Cohort / Batch: 82319
22 21 20 19 18 ● 5 4 3 2 1

Rosie and Mr. Spooks

Story by
Alexa Tuttle

Illustrated by
Carlie Tuttle

WonderCorp
EST 2018

Las Vegas, NV
www.wondercorp.fun

It's Halloween night and Rosie is done,
curled up on the couch after having such fun.

She loves the fall weather, the smell of the air,
and the breeze through the window that rustles her hair.

"The only thing missing," she thinks all alone,
"is someone to share with this feeling of home."

She puts on a movie. She's cozy and warm,
while outside it drizzles. She loves a good storm.

Wrapped up in her blanket, she's safe in her chair.

Then something-- it shocks her!

She JUMPS with a scare!

Rosie is frozen.

What should she do?

Should she smack down the spider, or tell it to shoo?

Just then the creature waves its small hand.
It plops in her cocoa–– so not what she planned!

A small scream slips out! She's flailing her arms!
She runs through the house filled with alarm!

Where can she hide from this critter so small?
She dashes to her bedroom and sits by the wall.

She waits in the corner...

She stares at the door...

She's rocking and shaking
all scared on the floor.

"You're acting so foolish.

It's just a small bug!

Get ready for bed
and get up off the rug!"

She carefully sneaks out into the hall.

Where could it be hiding?

The ceiling?

The wall?!

"I don't think it's in here...
Whew!" Rosie thinks.
"Uh oh... what's that there?"
She turns and she blinks.

"It's just a shadow," she says to herself.

She runs in the bathroom and past the bookshelf.

Rosie grabs her toothbrush and cleans all her teeth.

She sees a dark object just out of her reach.

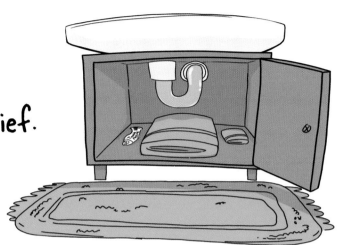

"It's just my towel!"

She sighs with relief.

She rinses her mouth out

and laughs, "Oh good grief."

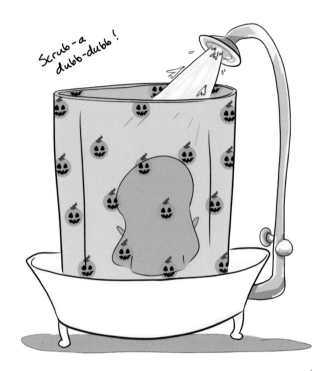

Into the shower,
scrub-a-dub-dub!

She keeps her eyes ope
defending the tub.

Soon she steps out,
all shiny and clean.

What's that in the corner?

A spider she's seen?!

"Oh, that's just my loofah!"
She laughs and gets dressed.

Loofah?!

"It's probably gone now,"
she says (slightly stressed!)

ha ha...

She sprints to her bedroom
and jumps in her bed.

She lays on her pillow
and next to her head...

The spider is waiting!

He's sitting right there!

She can't move a muscle as he climbs on her hair!

She SWATS him away and runs out of the room!
She darts down the hall super fast-- zip, zap, zoom!

She races to the kitchen and stands on a chair.
But to her surprise, the spider is there!

"What do you want?!" she screams while she runs.
"Just leave me alone. This game isn't fun!"

She crawls in the closet at the end of the hall.

She's crouched on her knees in the cupboard so small.

She shakes, filled with fear.
She senses him near.

She turns on the light
and cries out, "Oh dear!"

The spider advances.
He's getting real close!

Rosie's afraid it wil
land on her nose.

Instead, he drops down, right onto a pile
of Halloween movies and gives her a smile.

"What's this?" she thinks, now practically mute.

The spider, so scary, is actually cute!

He picks out a movie, her favorite one,
with the carefully crafted web that he spun.

"I can't believe this... You want to watch, too!"
She says with a smile. He nods, "Yes, I do."

She picks him up gently and carries him out.
She puts in the movie and sits on the couch.

They share Rosie's treats as the scary film plays.
Rosie thinks, "What an interesting end to this day."

"I think I'll call you my friend, Mr. Spooks,"
she says with a grin. (What a couple of kooks!)

They curl up together, Rosie and her new friend,
enjoying their Halloween moment.

Alexa Tuttle

Carlie Tuttle

Hi there! My name is Alexa.
I am a writer, filmmaker, storyteller, and big sister.
My favorite snack is apples, my favorite outfit is pajamas and my favorite holiday is HALLOWEEN!
I wrote this book to share with others my love for the spooky season and my realization that sometimes things aren't as scary as they seem.

Hello, I'm Carlie!
I love to draw and play videogames. My sister, Alexa, likes apples, but I like crunchy green grapes.
When I'm not drawing, I love to play with my puppies and exercise outside.
Drawing Rosie on her adventures is a blast because she's very expressive and always seems to be getting into trouble!

If you love Rosie as much as we do, check out our website:

www.wondercorp.fun

You can sign up for our e-newsletter to learn about Rosie's other adventures!